Going to New Orleans to Visit
Weezie Anna

*A Child's Eye View
of the Unique Phrases and Places of
the Crescent City*

Written and Illustrated by Mary Beth Pisano

QUAIL RIDGE PRESS

DEDICATION

For my Carmen, Joey,
Melissa, Lauren, and Abigail . . .
I love you so.
And a special thanks
to my dad, BK, always.

First Printing: December, 1994
Second Printing: March, 1996
Third Printing: September, 1999

Library of Congress Cataloging-in-Publication Data

Pisano, Mary Beth.
    Going to New Orleans to visit Weezie Anna / by Mary Beth Pisano.
        p.   cm.
    "A Child's eye view of the unique phrases and places of the Crescent City."
    Summary: When a little girl hears about her upcoming trip to New Orleans, Louisiana, she tries to imagine a place with snowballs in the summer, king cakes, and shotgun houses.
    ISBN 0-937552-52-6 : $8.95
    [1. English language—Terms and phrases—Fiction. 2. New Orleans (La.)—Fiction. 3. Afro-Americans—Fiction. 4. Stories in rhyme.]
I. Title.
PZ8.3.P5586835Go 1993
[E]—dc20   93-34203
                                                              CIP
                                                              AC

QUAIL RIDGE PRESS
P. O. Box 123   Brandon, MS 39043
1-800-343-1583
Printed in Canada

Way down yonder
in *New Orleenz*,
Lives a little girl
in polka-dot jeans.

Her name is Weezie Anna
and she's five years old.
She lives in a *shotgun house*—
at least that's what I'm told.

She told me all about herself
and about *The Crescent City.*
It sounds kind of strange to me,
but Weezie says it's pretty.

Weezie Anna's daddy
has a funny job, you see,
for every day a *ferry*
takes him across the Mississippi.

Beyond the *CBD*
where the buildings all get shorter,
Weezie Anna's daddy
has an office *in the Quarter*.

Weezie Anna told me
that her mommy's busy, too.
But once in a while they find time
to *pass by* the zoo.

Her mommy spends some time
making groceries during the day.
How does Weezie Anna's mommy do that?
I really couldn't say.

The food that Weezie Anna eats
sounds rather strange to me.

Dirty rice and *mud bugs?*
Now these I've got to see!

And sandwiches made on long, long bread?
I never would have guessed
that when you order one, they ask,
"You want your *sandwich dressed?*"

Square donuts called *beignets*
are served with cups of *café au lait*.
I'd like to see their *king cakes*
that sometimes rule the day.

Fat Tuesday is the day she says
I really shouldn't miss.
Beads and throws, floats and masks...
Please, tell me what's all this?

Weezie explains that *Mardi Gras*
is a big party in the street,
and that she *catches parades* sometimes.
Boy, does that sound neat!

Weezie Anna says we'll go uptown
to ride a big *streetcar*.

She says it's always loads of fun,
and it can take us far.

We'll get to see *Lee's Circle*
and also *Jackson's Square*.
I'm getting so excited
just to think of going there!

We'll get to see the *Superdome*,
the biggest marvel yet—
where they play ballgames in the rain
and nobody gets wet.

Weezie Anna is my friend
who I'm going to see real soon.
It should be quite an adventure
in *a city shaped like the moon*,

Where everything sounds different
from any place I've been.
And whoever are those *Saints*
who keep on *marching in*?

GLOSSARY

A brief explanation of New Orleans expressions, customs, and landmarks mentioned in the book.

Big EZ—An abbreviation for one of New Orleans' nicknames. "The Big Easy" refers to the laid-back, easy life-style of its residents.

blues—A soulful type of music played and sung in many of the music clubs in the city.

café au lait—Coffee with milk.

catch a parade—Slang for "going to a parade."

CBD—Central Business District. The buildings are tall in the CBD, but building restrictions don't allow tall buildings in the French Quarter.

Crescent City—A popular nickname for New Orleans because of the big bend in the Mississippi River on which the city is located. It is a *city shaped like the moon.*

dirty rice—A delicious south Louisiana rice dish made with chicken livers, vegetables and spices.

Fat Tuesday—Mardi Gras is French for Fat Tuesday. It is very appropriate since the next day is Ash Wednesday, the beginning of the Lenten season.

ferry—The reference is to one of the several ferry boats which crosses the Mississippi River.

Jackson Square—A lovely park located between the St. Louis Cathedral and the French Market. A statue of Andrew Jackson on his horse is in the center of the square. It is considered the heart of the French Quarter.

jazz—Rhythmic, play-it-like-it-feels music by a group of musicians playing instruments together.

king cake—An icing-covered coffee-type cake served widely during the carnival season (approximately from early January until Mardi Gras day). The cakes are baked with a tiny Kewpee doll or bean in them. At a King Cake party, the guest who gets the piece of cake with the baby or bean in it must give the next party.

Lee Circle—An impressive monument dedicated to General Robert E. Lee. The road circles around the statue at the downtown intersection of St. Charles Avenue and Howard Avenue.

Mardi Gras—A big costume-party-parade celebration the last day before the fasting of Lent begins.

making groceries—A rather unique New Orleans expression for shopping for groceries.

mudbugs—A common term for crawfish. They are considered a delicacy in south Louisiana.

New Orleenz—Slang for New Orleans.

pass by—A widely used term for "go to," as in "I'm going to *pass by* your house."

Quarter—The French Quarter, or Vieux Carré, is a section of old New Orleans world renowned for its music, art, food, and restored charm.

Saints keep marching in—Words taken from the old-time spiritual "When the Saints Go Marching In." Today it is most widely used in reference to the New Orleans Saints NFL football team.

sandwiches dressed—The term for a sandwich ordered with mayonnaise, lettuce and tomatoes. The usual order is, for example, "a roast beef sandwich, dressed."

shotgun house—A 1900's style of New Orleans house so named because the rooms are one behind the other. It was said that a bullet fired from a shotgun through the front door would pass out through the back door.

sno ball—A summer-time treat made of shaved ice and flavored syrups. There are 500-700 stands in the New Orleans area. In days gone by, sno balls were sold from trucks and horse-drawn wagons.

streetcar—These are usually called trolleys by tourists. Currently, the St. Charles line is the oldest continuously operating streetcar line in the USA.

street musicians—Musicians who play on street corners and sidewalks for donations from passersby.

Superdome—A gigantic dome-shaped covered stadium/coliseum used for big sports and entertainment events.

Weezie Anna—A sweet little girl named for her home state, Louisiana.

About the Author / Illustrator . . .

Mary Beth Pisano has always had a love for writing and drawing. Born in New Orleans, she lived for a time in Florida, then moved back to Marrero just across the river from New Orleans. She and her husband and four children have been experiencing life in different parts of the country due to his job with the Air Force. "We will always be a Southern family no matter where we travel—I've even learned how to make homemade beignets which really helps when we are homesick for New Orleans!"